Willow

Norm Bomer

watercolor illustrations by Stan D. Myers

Baker Books

A Division of Baker Book House Co
Grand Rapids, Michigan 49516

Published by Baker Books
a division of Baker Book House Company
P.O. Box 6287, Grand Rapids, MI 49516-6287

Printed in the United States of America

Library of Congress Cataloging-in-Publication Data

Bomer, Norm.
    Willow / Norm Bomer ; watercolor illustrations by Stan D. Myers.
        p.   cm.
    Summary: Willow the rabbit thinks that she would rather be free than well cared for and loved by Rebecca and Benjamin, but when she does escape from her hutch she finds that her home is best just the way God planned it.
    ISBN 0-8010-4362-X (cloth)
    [1. Rabbits—Fiction. 2. Freedom—Fiction. 3. Christian life—Fiction.] I. Myers, Stan D., ill. II. Title.
PZ7.B636545wi   1998
[E]—dc21
                                   97-39857
                                        AC

For current information about all releases from Baker Book House,
visit our web site:
http://www.bakerbooks.com/

Dedicated with love
to my wife, Carol,
and our children,
the real Rebecca and Benjamin

With special thanks to
Jane Whitman,
one of the best friends
Willow ever had

Willow wanted to get out. She wasn't happy.

She didn't whine about it. She simply felt sorry for herself. Sometimes, she even felt angry.

Willow surely would have whined. But she couldn't. Bunnies can't whine. They can only hop about and keep to themselves.

There was one big reason for Willow's unhappiness. What was it?

Was she unhappy with her food? Not really. In fact, she was quite well fed.

Every day, Rebecca brought her fresh water. And she gave Willow a generous helping of crunchy nuggets.

Those nuggets were delicious! They weren't plain old rabbit food pellets either. They were the same crunchy nuggets that Beau ate every day. That made them even more special.

Beau was the big black dog who lived in the yard. His real name was Beauregard. But everyone called him Beau.

Willow was scared to death of Beau. Sometimes, he would sniff the ground around her hutch. Then he would push his nose right against the wire screen and stare at her.

Perhaps deep down inside he wanted to eat her. Dogs do eat bunny rabbits sometimes.

Or perhaps deep down inside he wanted to be friends. "I doubt that!" Willow thought to herself.

Perhaps Beau was just jealous about the crunchy nuggets. After all, they were from *his* food sack! They were supposed to be for big dogs like him. Why should this little white bunny have them?

Willow liked the idea of making Beau jealous. It made her food taste even better. She would hop smartly to the end of her hutch and nibble a few nuggets. Beau would just keep staring.

Then he'd mosey away, stopping once or twice to look back at the hutch. Finally, he'd turn around a few times under the tulip tree and plop down with a long sigh. With his chin on his paws he'd stare across the yard at the hutch.

Willow had many other good things to eat too.

Now and then, Rebecca would bring a large box of lettuce leaves from the market. Her little brother, Benjamin, would hold open the hutch door, and she would reach in with a pile of that sweet, juicy lettuce!

While Rebecca was at school, Benjamin often visited the hutch with special treats like broccoli or carrots or celery or fresh dandelions.

No, food wasn't Willow's problem.

Well, then. What was the problem?

Was Willow unhappy with her home? Not really. In fact, she had quite a lovely home.

Her hutch was nestled under a big pine tree next to the wood pile. The fence near the hutch door was twined with roses and honeysuckle. And beside her bed God had placed the flowering branches of a dogwood.

On some fine days, Rebecca and Benjamin would put Beau in his dog pen and leave Willow's hutch door open. Those days were wonderful—even for an unhappy bunny.

She would hop this way and that way, sniffing and sniffing and sniffing and sniffing. She would sniff the fence, sniff the grass, sniff the trees. She would sniff the swing, sniff the sandbox, sniff the gate.

She would sniff the back porch, the back door, the broom, and Benjamin's tricycle.

She would even sniff Benjamin! And Rebecca!

Sniff, sniff, sniff! She was free!

Often she would sniff out some tasty greens, and her sniffing would change to munching. Then she would sit on her haunches and make a big show of washing her face and grooming her long ears.

Sometimes, with no warning, Willow would tear across the grass and jump high, twisting around and kicking her strong bunny legs in the air.

Willow didn't look unhappy. The truth is, on those fine days, she didn't feel too unhappy either.

No, Willow's home wasn't the problem. But just the same she was unhappy most of the time.

What was the big problem?

Was it Willow's family perhaps? Was Willow not loved?

Oh, no! That was not the problem.

There was so much loving care! There were flowers and food and freedom and a safe hutch.

And there were all those cuddles and hugs and kisses!

Oh, yes! Rebecca gave Willow more than lettuce and water! She gave plenty of back pats and gentle ear rubs too.

And that's not all. Many times, she invited Willow to play house. She wrapped her in baby blankets and snuggled her and talked to her sweetly. She gave her rides in the wagon and even took her into her own bedroom for tea parties.

Benjamin also gave Willow much more than broccoli and dandelions. Often he went to the hutch with no food at all. He opened the door and gently lifted Willow out. Benjamin was just tall enough for that! He sat there stroking Willow's silky white fur and hugging her in his arms.

All that loving was better than any crunchy dog food!

No, Willow's family wasn't the problem. Her family loved her very much!

The problem was Willow.

You see, on the outside she was white as a dogwood blossom and soft as a rose petal. But on the inside she was selfish.

Willow ❦❧ 15

Her home and loving family were not enough for
Willow. She wanted more. She wanted to get out—all the
way out—out of the hutch and out of the backyard too.

Willow was tired of being told what to do. She wanted
to make up her own mind. She wanted to choose her own
food. She wanted to sniff where *she* decided to sniff.

She did not want to be put back into her hutch by
Rebecca or Benjamin. She wanted to stay out all night if she
felt like it.

And she wanted to get away from that old Beau once
and for all. She was tired of his staring. Who did he think
he was, anyway?

To sum it up, Willow wanted to be free. Completely free! One autumn night, and long after the smell of honeysuckle had left the air, Willow sat in the dark thinking unhappily, "Why did God make me this way? Why did he put me here?

"I want to be like the wild bunnies," she thought. "They do whatever they please!"

At that, Willow gave the hutch door an angry bump.

With a tiny rattle, the door swung open. Benjamin had forgotten to close the latch!

Willow was surprised, but she didn't wait a minute! She poked her head out into the yard and hopped to the grass below.

The ground was covered with big leathery yellow leaves from the tulip tree and little shriveled red leaves from the dogwood.

At the sound of the dry leaves Willow froze like a statue. But her little heart didn't freeze. It danced like rain-drops on the flat roof of her hutch. She was suddenly very frightened.

"Where is Beau?" Willow asked herself. Inside the hutch she hadn't thought about that big dog, Beau.

There she sat, stock still. Willow was free. But so far, the freedom didn't feel really wonderful. There was no one around to put Beau in his pen.

The yard was quiet. The house was dark. And some-where Beau was fast asleep. "I hope so!" thought Willow.

Willow was good at spinning around. Now was a good time to do it.

With a swoosh through the leaves she spun and made a hoppity run to the back corner of the fence. There she stopped and listened again. No Beau!

It didn't take long for Willow to paddle away some dirt

with her sharp claws. In a moment, she had scooped a hole
right under the fence.

In another moment, Willow was free. Really free, she thought.

Being outside the fence felt wonderful! The air was cool and spiced with the cinnamon of autumn leaves.

Of course, the air was the same in the backyard. But it seemed so much sweeter mixed with freedom.

The moon shone bright, and it was very late. But that little white bunny wasn't at all sleepy. She was too excited to be sleepy.

She sat for a short time soaking in the freedom.

To her left was the thick shadow of the woods. To her right, down the hill a bit, was the road.

Straight ahead was the clover field. Many times, Willow had dreamed of going there.

She darted across a tiny meadow and stopped at the edge of the clover.

Sniff, sniff. Sniff, sniff.

There was the clean smell of soil and the woody odor of stubble. But the summer perfume of clover blossoms was long gone. And the last green scent of the leaves had been cut and hauled away.

There sat the free little bunny, very white in the moonlight, thinking about clover. And thinking about freedom.

"How I would love to munch a few juicy purple clover blossoms right now!" she wished. "Or even some sweet, tender clover leaves."

Just then, Willow heard a far-away jingling sound.
Jingle, jingle.

Maybe it wasn't so far away.

Jingle, jingle. Jingle, jingle. It was louder now. Then she
remembered. She had heard that sound many times before.
But it had never concerned her.

Things were different tonight. Jingle, jingle, jingle! It was the sound of dog collars. Two of them. Coming closer.

Wearing one collar was a black Labrador with a wide head and black eyes. Wearing the other was a collie dog with long hair and long teeth. Willow had watched those two many times in the past.

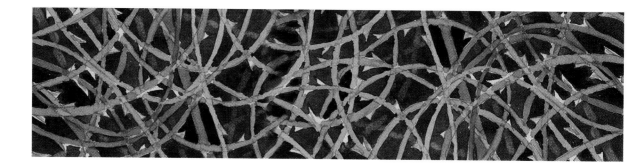

With keen noses and growling bellies they were hunting rabbits.

"Quick!" thought Willow. "The fence!"

Like a bumpity white arrow, she flew toward the backyard fence. But where was the hole?

Back and forth, back and forth she bounced in panic. But the hole under the fence was gone.

Like two dark eagles, the dogs swooped in for the kill. But Willow was very fast. Through the moonlight and into the dark woods she flashed with the shrill whine of the dogs close behind.

The underbrush was woven tightly with briars and thorns. The lab and the collie were stopped short. But Willow scrambled deep into the thicket.

The brambles tore her skin and grabbed painfully at her legs. She stumbled and twisted, leaving white tufts of fur on the thorns.

Soon she was safe—at least for a while. And she was still free. She was also still quite unhappy. In fact, she was more

unhappy than ever before. She was hurting and she was very
afraid. She was terribly thirsty too.

The fresh water in her hutch crossed her mind. Then she
thought of Rebecca and all those cuddles and hugs. She
thought of Benjamin's little arms around her neck.

Perhaps bunnies can't really cry. But Willow began to cry
in her own bunny way. She wanted to go home.

All night, she sat motionless in the dark thicket. The
jingle, jingle of the dogs had disappeared. The scratches and
the cuts and the fear were all still there.

At the first faint light of dawn, Willow tried to move.
She didn't know how far into the thicket she had scampered.

Carefully, painfully, she headed out, one hop at a time. If

she could only get back to the fence. She was sure she could find the hole this time.

There were even more cuts and scratches by the time she reached the edge of the wood. There was the fence. There was the backyard. There was home.

All was quiet. Slowly she crept along the edge of the meadow to the corner of the fence. The hole was still there after all.

She was sore all over. Even so, she was under the fence in an instant.

And in an instant, there was Beau. It seemed he had been waiting for her.

Beau had sniffed the fence and found the small hole. Now he had found Willow.

She sat there without moving, and Beau just stared. Then he stepped slowly toward her.

By instinct she sprang away but stopped just as suddenly. Again Beau stepped toward her and timidly stretched his neck in her direction.

Her heart beat wildly. Everything else was quite calm. Even Beau. Something was wrong. He could tell that much.

"I can't run anymore," Willow decided. "I don't want to run away anymore."

She just sat there as Beau sniffed this side and that, very carefully and at a safe distance. No, he wasn't going to eat her after all.

He backed away and went to the tulip tree to lie down.

With relief and great tiredness, Willow crawled slowly along the back fence and lay down under the hutch.

When the sun was at last shining brightly, two loving children found a calm white bunny rabbit under the hutch in their backyard. She was rather shaggy and quite dirty. But she was happy just the same.

Rebecca wrapped her in a blanket as green as clover. Benjamin got some fresh water. And he brought some chunky nuggets from the dog food sack.

From that day on, Willow was the happiest bunny in any backyard anywhere. She was free from that awful fear of being torn apart by strange dogs. She was free from sitting hungry in dead clover fields. She was free from hiding in perfectly awful briar thickets.

I guess you could say she was just plain free.

Rebecca and Benjamin usually left the hutch door wide open after that. They knew Willow would be safe—even with Beau in the yard. She wouldn't try to run away. And Beau's staring didn't hurt one bit.

Willow even got so brave as to hippity-hop right up to him one day. He just lay there under the tulip tree, and she sniffed him right on his ear.

Now that little white rabbit and that big black Doberman can often be seen lying together in the grass. It makes some people think of the lion and the lamb lying down together in God's eternal kingdom. (God did make families very special!)

But it is just Willow and Beau in their own backyard. It is a home like many other homes. It is a family like many other families.

There are rules. There are fences. There are selfish feelings too. Sometimes there is downright grouchiness.

There are also flowers and food. And there is freedom—just the right kind of freedom. It is tied with strings of love.

Willow has found exactly what she always wanted.

  Willow